THE SECRET
OF MISTY MOUNTAIN

By L. Michelle Bowen

THE SECRET
OF MISTY MOUNTAIN

By L. Michelle Bowen

Purple Finch Press
20 Lakeview Drive
Northwood, NH 03261

Printed in the United States of America.

LCCN: 2019912204
ISBN-13. 978-1-5450-7000-0

Visit: www.lmichellebowen.com

_____

Dedicated to my children, Jake, Alex and Zach
who make story-telling my greatest joy.

_____

Table of Contents

CHAPTER 1
Aunt Bessie Comes to Town

"FRIED CHICKEN," I heard my mama yell. "FRIED CHICKEN, I SAID! F... R... I... E... D... CHICKEN! You better get your bottom out of that bed right now if you want some."

Up from my bed I jumped. I couldn't believe it! Fried chicken….and for breakfast?

It was breakfast time, right? I looked out the window and saw that the sun was just coming up. It was going to be a bright, warm day, for sure. Mama knows fried chicken is my favorite thing in the world to eat. And it's Saturday. I bet Mama did it to make sure I'd wake up. She knows I'd rather stay tucked up tight under my warm blanket than get up early on a Saturday morning.

Down the stairs I ran. I almost tripped over my nightgown. It's my favorite nightgown with red and green plaid, short sleeves and lace at the bottom with a matching cap. The cap is there to keep my hair from going everywhere. Mama says my hair is a holy mess. She made the cap and nightgown for me to match my dolly I got for Christmas. Her name is Isabelle. I know 8th grade girls aren't *supposed* to play with dolls anymore, but I know we all secretly still do. As I ran into the kitchen and stopped dead in my tracks. It dawned on me that I did not smell fried chicken. I looked over at Mama and she gave me a smile and a wink and said, "Hey there, sleepy head."

"Mama," I said, "Where's the fried chicken?"

"Right here," she replied. All I saw was a frying pan with eggs in it, a plate next to it with some biscuits and bacon and grits in a bowl.

"Where?" I asked.

"Right here in this frying pan," Mama giggled.

"MAMA! That's fried eggs!!!!"

"Eggs come from chickens, right Anne? It is my understanding that eggs have chickens in them. Well, at least sorta?" Mama did that big belly-laugh she always does when she cracks herself up. I've never heard her laugh like that when anyone else says something funny, only when she says something funny. I rolled my eyes at Mama and just sat down at the breakfast table. "Aww, precious, you look as sad as an umbrella in a drought. Now, now, baby. Don't you go getting all huffy at me. I had to get you up somehow. I knew you'd never come down if you heard me say it was time to get up to greet your Aunt Bessie when she arrives."

Aunt Bessie... I forgot all about her coming to visit. She was Mama's oldest (and plumpest) sister – older by ten years. My Nana had eight children and Mama was the youngest. Aunt Bessie was kind of like a second mama to my mama. We always had to be spiffy and polite when Aunt Bessie visited, which wasn't very often. "Mind your manners," Mama would say, "I don't want your Aunt Bessie thinking I ain't given you some good raisin'."

It was about this time that I saw my brother sliding around the corner with a HUGE smile on his face. "Fried chicken! Honest?" Frank was three years older than me (well, two and a half to be specific) and a whole lot taller! Everyone says we look alike, but I don't see it at all. Frank is tall and lanky and he kinda looks like a praying mantis when he walks with his gawky arms. Frank also has very thick jet-black hair.

I, on the other hand am not very tall at all. And, while I am a little lanky, I don't walk around flapping my elbows everywhere when I walk. Also, I have long, thin brown hair. Nothin' like Frank at all, I tell ya. Nothin'.

Once again, Mama gave that evil grin and wink. This time to Frank. He sulked down into his chair, just like I did. After a little bit of poutin', me and Frank scarfed down our *fried chicken*. I added some honey-butter to my biscuits. Mama made the best biscuits this side of the Mason-Dixon line. At least that's what I was always told. I don't even know what the Mason Dixon line really is. Anyways, most folks like their biscuits fluffy, but our family likes them thin and flat. That way you can put all kinds of stuff on them evenly, which I did a lot. But Mama's homemade honey-butter, now that was the best.

After breakfast, me and Frank got all gussied up and went with Mama and Daddy to the train station to get Aunt Bessie. I always liked going to the train station because it was a chance to go into town. We didn't go as much as I would have liked. It wasn't easy being poor, but we got by. Don't get me wrong, we had food and a roof over our heads. Shoot, we even had some land, a cow, two goats and six chickens. But we struggled from time to time and doing extra things was a rare event in the Childers family. So, you can see why I was excited to get out and go into town.

The train station always seemed to be busy with people in such a hurry. Folks would walk past you without even looking at your face or saying a single word. Not even "Hey". We passed the ticket booth and the colored waiting area where black folks waited for their people to get off the train. We've come a long way in Bent Creek, South Carolina. We allow colored folk to come into the train station like the rest of us. We even have special bathrooms for them. They don't have to go somewhere else now. Mama says it's a big step for most Southerners to open any doors to colored people – even if it's not the doors they, themselves use. I have no idea what that means, but I wondered what it would be like if I was the girl who had to sit in the back or go to a separate place all the time. I'm pretty sure that *some* doors might not quite be enough. But that's how things were and how they were going to be, especially here in the South. Coloreds were allowed many things that once was kept from them, but they most certainly were not allowed to share things like water fountains and bathrooms and stuff like that. They had their own of those things and it seems to be working out just fine if you ask me.

We made it to the drop-off area as the train was pulling in. The train was huge and louder than I had expected it to be. When it was stopping, I thought my ears were going to explode right then and there. The brakes just squealed along the track causing a sound that would burst a dog's eardrums. I had to throw my hands up and cover my ears tightly. I looked up and saw that Frank was doing the same thing. Sometimes we do things so much alike, it's like we're twins. But other times, I wonder if Mama found him on the side of a dirt road somewhere. Like wolves had left him behind or something.

The train stopped and we began to look for Aunt Bessie. I kept trying to be the first to see her, but Mama was too excited, and she kept moving in front of me. Finally, I saw Aunt Bessie get off the train. She had the biggest grin on her face. She was wearing a black dress with red and white flowers all over it. She had a beautiful white hat with a tiny lace dropping in the front. Aunt Bessie may have been a little bit big, but she always looked her best. She plopped down off the train and I heard Mama yell, "Well, I declare, you look as pretty as a silver dollar!" Mama loved comparing people to things. I really don't know why, but she did it a lot!

"Darlin, I've missed you like a preacher misses Sundays." Apparently, Aunt Bessie liked to compare things, too. I watched Mama and Aunt Bessie hug and cry and just hold each other. It was obvious they had missed each other greatly. I wonder if Frank and I will love each other like that when we grow up. Then Mama and Aunt Bessie let go of each other and began to shout a lot of things back and forth. I have no idea what they were saying, but I know Mama was just as happy as she could be. Aunt Bessie hadn't been able to visit in two years. It's been hard for her to come down from Ohio since her husband died. But now she was here, and Mama was in her happy place.

CHAPTER 2
The Stranger in the Woods

We waited a while for the conductor to get Aunt Bessie's bags off the train, then Daddy had Frank help him put the bags in the back of the car. Now Daddy, that's who Frank looked exactly like. They were both tall, had arms and legs for miles and had the most piercing eyes you'd ever seen. But Daddy was a lot quieter and a lot more serious than Frank. He didn't smile very often. Daddy always took life very seriously and, in that way, Frank was nothing like him. Daddy always said Frank would *grow into* that part, but Frank said he hoped he never did. Frank was also a lot like Mama, laughing all the time and being silly. I liked that part of him.

After Daddy and Frank put the bags in the back of the station wagon, we headed home. Aunt Bessie sat in the middle of me and Frank and we had to endure hearing her and Mama practically scream every word they said to each other. Back roads could get loud and we had the windows down because it was so muggy and humid this time of year. But at least, since we were moving so fast down the road, we didn't have to deal with gnats or skeeters. That's the worst thing ever. I just let the wind blow straight through my hair. Didn't matter much anyways. My hair was like a rat's nest, even without the wind. Mama says chickens could lay their eggs in it and they'd be just fine.

The road home from the train station is a long one. We took many short, paved streets in the city, but once you get out in our neck of the woods, it gets bumpy, dirty and noisy. And it's one long back road to get to our house. We live on a plot of land that my great-grandfather left to my grandpa and he left it to my daddy. I guess Frank will get the land when he grows up. It's about ten acres and Daddy likes to keep as much of it woods as possible. He always said, "Why would I mess with the beautiful way God created it? It keeps us warm in the winter and cool in the summer." Frank says that when he grows up, he's going to farm it and make millions of dollars. He said he'd never be as boring as Daddy.

We pulled up to our little square cleared area, about an acre, where the house sat with a tiny barn, shed and chicken coop. Daddy gathered Aunt Bessie's bags and Mama and Aunt Bessie just walked on into the house cackling like two hens about to lay eggs at the same time. Frank ran off to the barn to play with one of our dogs, Patch. I was going to go in with Mama and Aunt Bessie when Daddy told me to run along and play so they could have some time. I took off to the woods with Spotty, our other dog. We worked real hard on the names of our dogs. Patch had brown patches all over his body while Spotty had little black spots on his. I figured why do them an injustice by naming them anything other than what they were? That's how they did it in the Bible – and that's the good Lord's word. So, we did just that and the dogs don't seem to mind at all.

Spotty and I ran to our favorite place in the woods down by the creek where the big oak tree fell. It got hit by lighting one year and landed itself perfectly across the creek. Spotty likes it here because he can play in the water and run around like he's just been set free. I like it because it's quiet and all mine. I walk back and forth over the big oak tree and sing and spin and make up stories that I tell to Spotty. I can be me and not have to pretend to be older or more responsible. It's my beautiful, secret hideaway where no one bothers me or picks on me or makes me do chores. I've spent many days down here by myself. I was raised by these woods and they are mine!

I was making up a story about a girl that ran away, but then felt sorry for it and was starting to miss her mama, but she was lost and was trying to figure out a way to get home. I heard some leaves rustle near me. That's not unusual to hear. There are many squirrels, rabbits, deer and birds all around. But this felt different and I jerked around to see what it was. There she stood. A total stranger. A girl in a pale blue flowered dress that stopped right at her knees. Her blonde hair was pulled in tight in a ponytail with a big pink bow and she was as clean as a whip. Her smile was as wide as any I'd seen on a girl and she had the most beautiful eyes I'd ever seen. Even more piercing than Frank's. And she was tall. Well, not super tall like Daddy and Frank, but much taller than me. We didn't speak for twenty minutes, or at least that's what it felt like. It was probably less than one minute, but still... We just stared at each other. Finally, I spoke up and said, "What are you doing here?"

"I was just taking a walk and heard a voice and came to see who it was. There's no crime in that, is there?"

Who is this stranger? What was she doing in my playground? I owned these woods. I claimed these woods when I was a little girl. She can't just go gallivantin' through them like they're hers now.

"Well, this is private property. And you are trespassin'. And tresspassin's a crime."

"I'm sorry. I didn't mean to make you angry. I'm new here and don't know my way around just yet. I was just looking for a place to play. I'm sorry I bothered you." Then she turned around and started to walk off.

It'd been years since I had someone to play with in the summer besides Frank and Spotty. I guess there's no harm in someone trying to have some fun and she didn't do anything wrong since she got lost. Shoot, why was I being so punchy about it anyways?

"Wait. Wait," I said. "I'm sorry. You just startled me. I'm not used to anyone being down here. Can we try this again and start over?

"Hey, my name is Anne."

"Hey back," she said, with a kind-of bounce in her voice. I didn't even know people's voices could bounce, but I swear, her voice bounced.

"I'm Catherine Singleton. It's a pleasure to meet you." Did she just say, "It's a pleasure to meet you?" I've never heard anyone under the age of thirty say that unless they were meeting an adult. She sure seemed all-fancy with her big way of talking and her pretty blue dress and her pinned-up ponytail with its big pink bow. I felt kinda dumb standing there with my simple clothes on. It was strange having a girl like her here in my woods. But why was she *really* here? I mean, was she really just taking a walk and got lost in nine acres of land? Maybe she was looking for someone. Maybe she ran away from home. There are lots of maybes I could think of.

"What are you doing here, really?" I blurted out.

"Oh, well we just moved here. We live right up there." She pointed to the top of the mountain where we were playing below. It's right at the outskirts of our land and about two million acres. I'd heard that, anyways. Up there's where the rich folks live. She must be rich. No wonder she looks so spiffy.

"Where did you move from?"

"Nashville. My daddy wanted us to move out to the country where he could have some privacy, so we did."

"Your daddy wanted it. Did you and your mama want to move, too?"

"My mama died two years ago," she said sadly. "And my daddy doesn't like living in the big city anymore. He says people know too much of his business and he wants us to lead a private life from now on."

"You mean, you don't have a mama around? I'm so sorry. That must be somethin' awful, to be sure. I don't know what I'd do. How do you get places? How do you buy clothes? How do you eat? Who do you talk to? Who washes your clothes?"

Catherine laughed and said, "Well, the same as everyone, I guess. I mean, we have Virginia and Harold. Virginia does all the cooking and cleaning and Harold takes me wherever I need to go. And so does my dad. Plus, Virginia is always there for me when I need someone to talk to. It's not like I'm stranded or starving."

I had heard about people who had hired help to do all their stuff, but I'd never met anyone who had them. I mean, my mama does all the cooking and cleaning. And what she doesn't do, she has me and Frank do. And my daddy does all the hard work on our little farm and drives us everywhere. Sometimes Mama will drive us, but she mostly likes to stay home. Daddy also works on people's tractors too. That's what Daddy does for money. He fixes tractors and some trucks.

"Well, Catherine," I said, "This is my favorite place to play in the woods. I play here almost every day. Maybe you and me can play some-time here if you want. We still have two months before school starts, we could play lots of fun stuff during that time. I mean, if you like that kinda thing."

"OK!" she shrieked. I love that she shrieked!

That was the beginning of the best friend-ship I've ever had in my whole entire life.

CHAPTER 3
The Tree House

_____

From that moment on me and Catherine were joined at the hip. We did everything together. She met my parents and Aunt Bessie. She met Frank and he made fun of her Saddle Oxford shoes. He actually made fun of a lot of things about her. Her ponytail, her laugh, her dresses. He was never mean, but he always picked on her. I would've hit him by now, but Catherine just laughed it off. She almost acts like she likes it sometimes. If a boy did that to me, I'd punch him in the nose. One day Frank and Catherine and me were swinging on the big tire and Frank kept on insisting that he be the person to push Catherine, and when he pushed her, he'd tug at her ponytail – every single time. Catherine would laugh, but I suspected she was just being nice. It would be very annoying for your best friend's brother to always tug at your ponytail and say silly things like, "Got it. Gonna keep it." She was a good sport at letting Frank tag along all the time. Aunt Bessie and Mama would just guffaw at the sight of it and not say a word. They would wink at each other and rock in their rocking chairs.

One day Catherine invited me to come to her house for dinner. It was a big blue house with white shutters and a huge front porch with four rockin' chairs on it, two of them with cushions. It had two front doors. Two! How would you even know which one to open? I was a little nervous to go inside. I'd never been in a house this big and fancy before. But Catherine acted as normal as ever and it made me feel comfortable.

Dinner was normal at Catherine's house. I'm not sure what I expected, but a pot roast, mashed potatoes, green beans, biscuits and peaches was not it. Don't get me wrong, Virginia was a good cook and all. But nothing would ever be as good as my mama's cooking. I mean, Virginia didn't even turn her pot roast broth into gravy. We didn't have gravy for our mashed potatoes. When I told my mama later about that, she laughed and reminded me that she was the Queen of all cooks. She's right.

At dinner, I finally got to meet Catherine's daddy plus Virginia and Harold. I found out that Harold was Virginia's brother and the only living family she has left. He didn't talk much. He just sat there and listened to all of us talk, kinda like my daddy. Virginia was so pleasant and asked me lots of questions. I really liked her from the start.

We spent a lot of time with Virginia. She was such a beautiful colored lady. She had the fullest cheeks and lips and she kept her hair perfectly done. She always stood up straight and spoke proper, like a white lady would. She was kind of like a mother to Catherine. She helped her with her hair, she gave her advice, and she picked out her clothes. I even caught them giggling together sometimes like they were friends. Yes, Virginia was definitely a great substitute for her mama being gone. They were lucky to have her.

She often would sit with us outside in the back yard while we were having a snack and tell us about her family and her life. We would sit on a blanket, soaking in the sun and drinking sweet tea while Virginia told us about life back in Tennessee. She had lost her parents at a young age and was raised by her Nana. That was her daddy's mama. She told us how Nana taught her to sew and to read and to think for herself. It was Nana that helped her get her job with Catherine's daddy. She held Catherine's hand and told her, "Your daddy was the kindest and most gentle man I had ever met in my life. He took care of me and my brother and I have never wanted for anything since."

I knew Virginia was so thankful to be working for such a great family.

Lots of times, I'd just watch Catherine with her. Virginia was always hugging Catherine and holding her hand and saying really sweet things to her. It's like having your own cheerleader, right there in your house. And also having someone to help you with your homework and cook really good food for you and laugh with you. I think Virginia is one of the nicest ladies I've ever met.

We played together most every single day that summer, 'cept Sunday. I wasn't allowed to play on Sunday. No one is allowed to play on Sunday in the South. That's the Lord's day. And apparently, the Lord does not want us to have fun on that day. It's meant for being serious. But Catherine and I didn't care because we had every day except that day. I can't imagine a better summer than that one. I had never had a friend to play with like that and I couldn't have been happier.

One day, we decided to seek out treasures in the woods. Aunt Bessie had been telling us about how people had been finding rare coins and gold in the woods, and that's how our adventure was born. Frank wanted to go along. He said a gentleman would never let two girls go all the way around the mountain without a guard. Frank can be so dumb. So off we went and forged our way up and down Misty Mountain.

As we were coming down the back side of the mountain, I heard some rustling near us in the leaves on the ground. I thought it was a squirrel or a bird, but then I heard Frank calmly but sternly say, "Don't move, y'all. It's a copperhead." We both froze in our spots.

"What do we do?" asked Catherine.

"Don't move, Catherine. I'll take care of you," replied Frank. Then he held her hand.

I just rolled my eyes about a mile in the back of my head. "Y'all don't worry about me, now,"

I said. They both just looked at each other and giggled.

Frank slowly bent down and picked up a stick and threw it to the other side of the snake, away from us. The snake slithered off to the side in the opposite direction from where we were.

"Wow, Frank!" I said. "That was genius!"

"Yes, Frank. Thank you so much. I'm so glad you came with us today. What would we have done without you?" said Catherine.

Frank just beamed a very big smile and started to walk on. He didn't let go of Catherine's hand until after he had taken three or four steps.

One morning when we were walking in the woods, Catherine mentioned that she wished we had a house of our own to sit and talk in whenever we wanted. Just for the three of us. No adults, no other friends, just us three. Franks eyes lit up. "Catherine," Frank said with a grin, "If a house is what you want, then a house is what you shall have."

"What?" Catherine asked.

"I will build you a house. We have all we need right here in front of us. I can build us a tree house and you and Anne can decorate it."

It was brilliant! We were so excited and began planning right away.

We decided to build it in the big oak tree in our back yard. Frank got all the wood and supplies and me and Catherine got all the decorations. Mama let us have a few mason jars, a couple of old pillows and some curtains she didn't use anymore. We would hand Frank the wood and nails as he hammered away, building our dream house.

One day it was particularly hot, and the humidity was pretty thick. Catherine went inside with Mama and Aunt Bessie and she got Frank a glass of lemonade and brought it out to him with a cold rag to wipe away his sweat and cool him down. They sat by each other and talked as if I wasn't there. Sometimes I worried that she might like Frank more than me. But then again, she spends most of her time with me and not Frank. She was probably just making sure he knew how much we appreciated him doing all the hard work on the tree house.

That tree house became a constant meeting point for us. We'd sit and talk about all kinds of things there. Our dreams, our fears, our regrets. We'd tell funny stories and eat snacks that

Virginia would send over with Catherine like mini-sandwiches and cheese cubes. And we'd sip on Mama's sweet tea or some lemonade. It became one of my most favorite places to be.

Once, Catherine and I were in the tree house by ourselves because Frank had run into town with Daddy to pick up some supplies and she started asking me more about Frank. She asked me if he'd ever been sweet on a girl.

"Ewwww," I said. "That's is the grossest thing I've ever heard in my life." Catherine just laughed at me.

"Why would you care, anyways?" I questioned.

"I...I...I don't," she stuttered.

"Catherine, do you need to tell me something?"

"Anne, stop making it bigger than it is. I'm just curious, that's all."

"Are you?"

There was no response.

Some days Catherine was just mysterious like that. It was part of what was so fascinating about her. You never really knew if you got the whole story or not.

We did so many fun things that summer, but we also talked, a lot! But, then again, so did Mama and Aunt Bessie. One day, we were all sitting on the front porch drinking some sweet tea when Aunt Bessie blurted out, "Did I ever tell you about the time your mama and me got in such a big fight that your mama packed up her clothes and ran away?

"No." I said. "You gotta tell us!"

"Don't listen to her, girls. She's an exaggerator by nature. She can't help but make things bigger than they really were," Mama said.

"Hush, girl. Let me talk," Aunt Bessie said as she winked at me and Catherine. "Well, it was when your mama was seven and I was seventeen. I had been planning for a month to go to the local dance at the dance hall with a couple of my girlfriends. I was so excited and almost ready to go when your mama came bursting into my room dressed to the nines. To the nines, I tell you. Fancy church dress, big bow in her freshly curled hair, best shoes on and some rouge on her cheeks and lips, which we weren't even allowed to do back then. And when I asked her if she was being a princess, she just smiled and sweetly said, "Nope. I'm going to the dance with you." Not only could we not have kids in the dance hall, but I had no intention of being escorted by my seven-year-old sister. So, I gently—"

"Gently?" mama yelled out. "Gently, my foot!"

"Hush! Yes, gently, I told her she couldn't go. Well, as you can imagine, that did not go over so well. She pitched a hissy so big that I think people in Texas could hear her. In the end, when I told her 'no' means 'no' and that was enough, she stormed out of my room, big 'ole crocodile tears in her eyes and slammed the door behind her. Well, I figured I'd make it up to her the next day. Maybe have some play time with her and pretend we were at the dance."

"Mama, I would have loved to see you throwing a fit like that. Ha-ha. That would have been hilarious!" I laughed.

"Hush child," Mama commanded.

Aunt Bessie continued, "Shortly after that, maybe 15 minutes or so, my friends showed up to take me to the dance. I even remember the car that we were driving. It was a red Ford sedan. We thought we were something. Anyways, we headed down the road and as we were driving, we saw a little girl walking down the edge with a bag in her hand. As we got closer, I realized it was your mama. We pulled over and tried to talk to her and get her to go back home so we could get on to the dance. I even promised her a dance the next day at home. But she wouldn't budge. She was having nothing of it. She was determined to leave home for people who cared. Then she walked off from us, good shoes and all, and kept on down the road. So, I gave up and we got in the car and we headed to the dance.

"Oh no, Aunt Bessie. Please tell me you didn't just leave her there." Catherine exclaimed.

"I most certainly did. But then I knew what I had to do. I had my friends drop me off around the bend and I stood there waiting for your mama as she rounded that corner. She had just been a-cryin'. When she saw me, she ran into my arms and we held each other tight. And then without saying a word, we both walked back home together. When we got there, Daddy was sitting in the front room and playing his banjo and before we knew it we had ourselves a grand 'ole dance right there in our tiny little house. What a time that was!"

"I've never forgotten what you gave up for me that night, Bess," Mama said with a lump in her throat.

"Oh shush, sug. It was nothin."

"It was everything."

They both had tears in their eyes. I love it when Aunt Bessie tells stories like that. She's one of the best story-tellers I've ever heard. I wonder if me and Frank will ever have stories like this to share with our kids.

I enjoyed having Aunt Bessie around during this time. She was always giving words of wisdom and sayings. It's one of my favorite things about her. Aunt Bessie got to know Catherine really good too. She liked Catherine a lot and kept telling me there was something peculiar and special about that girl. I didn't know what that meant, but I was sure glad to have my Aunt Bessie and my best friend Catherine around. It felt like life just couldn't get any better than it was at that moment.

That was one of the coolest summers we'd had in a long time. That made it easier for us to play all the time. We weren't dying from the humidity. Not that you have to worry about that as much in the mountains. I think the trees and the wind kind of fight off the wetness a bit for you, so you can play from mornin' to night. And we did. All of us. Me and Catherine and Frank and the dogs made a whole lifetime of playing and living that summer in those woods. Honestly, I never played with Frank so much before that time. I guess it took having another friend around to bring him out of his hiding. He always asked me what we were doing and where we were going. And then he'd say, "I guess I can tag along to make sure y'all are safe and don't do nothin' dumb. Don't forget the copperhead."

CHAPTER 4
Back to School

_____

B ut all things must come to an end and it was time for school to start again. Catherine was very nervous about school and I told her not to be.

"School is nothing but a chance to get smarter while playing with your friends." I informed her of my friends, Margaret, Penny and Cheryl. We all sat together at lunch and talked about the cute boys. Cheryl was really my best friend out of that group. She and I were a lot alike and had done many things together. I knew Catherine would like her. I wasn't so sure if she would like Margaret and Penny, however.

Catherine and I decided that we would walk together to school since it was only a mile if we met in the middle of our houses. And that's just what we did. It gave us lots of talk time. Catherine told me all about her old school in Nashville and how she had more than one teacher and more than one classroom to go to. We didn't have that out here in our small town, but Catherine didn't seem to mind. She said, "It'll do me some good to get to keep with the same people all day long." I had no idea what that meant, but I agreed with her anyways.

"Yep, it'll do you some good, for sure," I said. Sometimes I find myself agreeing with people just to not look stupid. I've got to work on that.

We got to school a little bit early on that first day of school. That's when I heard someone yell across the way, "Well, I'll be a monkey's uncle, but if somebody I know didn't go out and get herself some new shoes!" I knew that voice without even turning my head. It was Margaret Pittman. She was always dressing herself up to be the prettiest, most modern girl at Bent Creek Junior High. She kept her blonde hair in all the current trends and made sure you knew it. I wondered who would notice my new Saddle Oxfords first. Of course, it was Margaret. Every year Mama and Daddy got me two new pairs of shoes and this year, I chose a pair of black sneakers for outside play and a pair of

Saddle Oxfords, very much like Catherine's, for school and church.

"Hey, hey Margaret. How was your summer?"

"The same as always. Visiting family, swimming at the beach, you know, boring stuff. "How was your summer?"

"It was great! My Aunt Bessie came to town over a month ago and will be staying with us for a few months. And I made a new friend who lives near me. Margaret, this is Catherine Singleton. She lives up on Misty Mountain, on the other side of the creek from us."

"Nice to meet you, Catherine. Oh, can we call you Katie for short?"

"Well, I don't know, I've never been asked that before," Catherine said.

About that time, Penny and Cheryl walked up and we hugged. We started to tell each other about our summers when Margaret took the liberty of introducing them to *Katie* as if I didn't even exist, as if I hadn't been the person to find Catherine, and as if Catherine didn't mind being called Katie. But I was used to Margaret. She always had to be the center of attention. I was OK with that because I really didn't like all eyes being on me anyways.

We went off to class and pretended to be interested while Mrs. Porter was teaching something about conjugating verbs. The lunch bell rang, and we all jolted for the courtyard. Our school had a small lunchroom that couldn't seat all the kids in school, so the rule was that if you brought your lunch, you were allowed to eat outside in the courtyard. I had already told Catherine to bring her lunch, so we were all ready to run past the cafeteria and head for the outside benches in the courtyard.

I pulled out my pimento cheese sandwich and carrots while Margaret opened her bag to reveal her turkey sandwich. Margaret was funny about her meat sandwiches. She used to always say that you had to have meat to make your skin smooth. Mama said that Margaret was so full of hot hair that it puffed her up. She said Margaret was a show-off with her words 'cause her brains had nothing to show for themselves. I don't know if that's true or not, but I was pretty sure turkey didn't make your skin look or feel better. Cheryl, Penny and Catherine also got out their sandwiches. But when Catherine took out her sandwich out, it looked weird and we all kind of stared at her.

"What?" she asked with a smile on her face.

"Why is your bread so brown?" I asked.

"It's wheat bread. Virginia makes it special for me. She says it's gonna help me grow up to be strong."

"Who is Virginia?" Penny asked.

"She lives with us. She's my friend," answered Catherine, almost apologetically.

Her friend? What does that even mean? I thought she was their housekeeper. She is, after all, a colored woman living in the quarters of their home. I'm not saying you can't be friends with a colored woman, but if they're living in your house, they're your help, right? Well, maybe Catherine just liked Virginia so much that she didn't want to speak down of her. Virginia did treat her as good as a mama would and that was very special, considering.

"What do you mean, your friend? Does your daddy have a woman living with him that's a friend?" said Margaret, sounding shocked. Faking being appalled, Margaret had a flair for the dramatics, and the big hair to go with it.

"Geez, Margaret. Stop being so dramatic," said Cheryl.

"No. That's not it," said Catherine, "She's not just help. She's, well, she's a part of my family. She's as good to me as my own mother was and she's my family." Catherine's tone was becoming harsher.

"Where exactly is your mama?" Margaret asked with accusation.

"In heaven," Catherine replied. Nobody said anything for a moment.

"Oh, I see. Well, is this Virginia a colored woman?" asked Margaret.

"Yes, she's black. So, what of it?"

"Oh," said Margaret. "Oh, ok. I get it. You have a fondness for your help."

"She's not a hired hand! She's family!" shouted Catherine.

"No need to get in a tizzy, now," sneered Margaret.

I immediately jumped in to defend her. "Catherine's mama died two years ago, and Virginia has been a great person to Catherine. She's filled in the void that Catherine was feeling without her mama around. She tends to her like our mamas tend to us."

Catherine jumped right in and said, "And she's family. That's all you need to know."

Everyone just stared at Catherine as she sat there, back straight, eyes wet, eating her egg salad sandwich on wheat bread. We didn't know what else to say. We really weren't even sure what just happened.

No one said anything else about it that day. No one except me, that is. But I saved my questions for later, after school.

CHAPTER 5
The BIG Secret

"Catherine," I began as we walked home from school, "Why did you get so upset during lunch over Margaret calling Virginia a hired hand?"

"I just did, Anne. That's all. She seemed like she was speaking down on Virginia and I won't have anyone speak down on my family."

"I understand that. And I agree. But I'm not sure she was speaking down on Virginia or your family. That brings up another question. I don't understand why you insist on calling her family. Don't get me wrong, I know she's as good as family to you, but you acted like it was so much more. It was kinda weird."

"Because, Anne, she really is family." Catherine stared into my eyes without moving a muscle.

"I don't understand," I said, honestly.

"Anne, I need to tell you something. I haven't told you this because I wasn't sure how you'd react. The whole reason we moved out of Nashville was because people weren't ready for what I'm about to tell you. It's the reason we live in the middle of nowhere. And if you repeat this, I'll surely die because people just aren't ready. You hear me, I'll surely die."

I was nervous. I had no idea what Catherine was going to say, and I felt a bit sick. "Ok, Catherine. You can tell me. You can tell me anything. You can trust me."

"Anne, Virginia is family. Actual family. She's family because she's... she's my daddy's wife."

Silence. There was no sound to be heard. Absolute silence. I was numb from the top of my head to the soles of my dirty feet. I kept trying to think if I might have heard wrong. If maybe she meant something else. But there were no ways to twist the words. *"Virginia is my daddy's wife."*

I can't even imagine how long Catherine and I stared at each other. I kept thinking: *Say something, Anne.* But no words came.

"Well, are you going to say something?" Catherine asked.

And there it was. I had to say something now.

"Well, I'm not sure what to say. I've never known someone married to a colored person before. This is all new to me. You've got to give me a second here, Catherine," I said. My head was spinning. I never really thought I'd have to think about this kind of thing.

"What? You're not going to run away calling me or my daddy a nigger lover?" Catherine asked, kind of in a nasty tone. Almost like she was challenging me. It hurt my feelings.

"Well, no. I'm not. First off, I think that nigger is a very silly word. I mean, what does that even mean, anyways? Second, Mama has always told me not to name-call people based on anything other than their own stupidity. And third, I really like Virginia. She is a sweet and kind person. So, no. I'm not going to run off and call names. But I do need a minute to soak all this into my skin. I mean, dang, Catherine."

"Well, thank you. You are the first friend I've had not to do that."

"Maybe I can see why. You did kind of throw it on me all at once and then yell at me like I did something wrong. But... if I think about it, there's probably no good way to say it, huh?"

"No. Not really."

We walked for a bit with no words between us. I kept trying to think of something to say, but I just didn't have the right words. I might not be a grown-up yet, but I do know enough to know that there is a time to talk and a time to shut your mouth. And I knew what time this was. So, I kept walking, shuffling my Saddle Oxfords in the leaves, mouth shut.

After a while, Catherine said, "Anne. Will you still be my friend like you were before? Now that you know the truth about my family, will you still be my best friend?"

"Catherine, that's a silly question. We are best friends. I don't think your daddy marrying someone should change that, even if she is a colored woman."

"It has for so many of my friendships. You have no idea, Anne. People have discarded me, humiliated me, hurt me, embarrassed me and said awful, horrible things to me. And even worse things to my daddy and to Virginia."

"I'm not those people, Catherine."

"Listen, Anne. You can't tell anyone what you know. I can't risk going through what I went through back in Nashville. I can't face another hurt like that. Promise me. Promise, Anne that you won't tell another living soul. Not even Frank. I will surely die if you tell anyone. I just don't think I could live through that kind of torture again."

"I swear, Catherine. I swear I won't tell anyone. Not Mama or Daddy. Not even Frank."

We were pretty much silent the rest of the walk home. I don't think either of us knew what to say next. She hugged me when it was time to part ways and told me that I was the truest friend she'd ever had.

I walked down the road feeling older, wiser and a much more confused than when this day began. How can you be more confused and wiser at the same time? I don't even know, but I was.

When I got home, Mama and Aunt Bessie bombarded me with questions. "How was the first day of school?" "Did you meet any new friends?" What's the new boy from Charleston like?" "How did Catherine like her new school?" "Did anything interesting happen today?"

The only question I really heard was, "Did anything interesting happen today?" Hmmm, anything interesting. Let me see. *Well, my best friend just now told me that the colored woman that I thought was her housekeeper is actually her daddy's wife and she's asked me to keep it as a secret for the rest of my entire life. Not to tell a single soul, not even my own mama! But other than that, no, nothing much to talk about.*

Of course, I didn't answer their questions directly. I told them that school was school. That I already had a new friend and didn't need to make another one. That I didn't get to meet the new boy from Charleston. That Catherine liked the school just fine, and the only interesting thing to happen was that Catherine eats brown wheat bread. Mama and Aunt Bessie just guffawed over that one.

"Why in the world would anyone need to mess with bread?" Mama laughed.

CHAPTER 6
Charles From Charleston

School was the same day after day. Margaret bossing everyone around and trying to get the new boy to notice her. Penny and Cheryl following her around like she carried a list of instructions saying, *"If you want to be popular, act like this."* But for me and Catherine, life was just grand. We played and laughed a lot. Catherine and I had many sleepovers and went to the woods practically every day after school once our chores and homework were done. Frank would often go with us. He and Catherine had a lot of the same humor and so I understood why he'd want to play with a couple of girls. Otherwise I would've been irritated at Frank for intruding. He and Catherine probably laughed more together than me and Catherine did most of the time.

Frank always made sure we had our girl time without him. That's when me and Catherine would sit and talk about serious stuff. Where we'd share our secrets. My secret was that I liked the new boy from Charleston. His name was Charles Henry. Charles from Charleston — how cute is that? His accent was so adorable, and to a thirteen-year-old girl, a boy with an accent is everything.

One day we were down by the creek, sitting on our log, (I had matured past playing on the log like a little schoolgirl. Now I was sitting and talking to my best friend about grown girl stuff) when we heard someone walking in our direction. We both turned and there he stood, handsome as ever. Charles from Charleston, right there in front of us, in our secret spot. Was God trying to tell me something? We grinned, he grinned and then Catherine elbowed me and giggled.

"Hey, y'all," Charles from Charleston said in his adorable accent. He had such a big smile on his face.

"Hey," we both said together.

"What'cha doin down here?"

"Just talking," Catherine said.

"Oh, neat. Can I sit and talk with you?"

"Sure," I said a little too eagerly.

So Charles from Charleston came down to sit with us and talk. With us! When he jumped over the creek and walked past me to sit by Catherine, my heart sank. I was so hoping he would have sat by me. But it didn't matter because I got to sit and listen to Charles from Charleston, with his adorable accent, tell us story after story of his shenanigans with his friends back home. How they'd steal candy at the market and chase each other along the Battery. Charles told us that the Battery is a park where a seawall is and lots of mansions. It was named for a civil-war battery. He also told us that he and his friends would go out in the ocean and find sand dollars.

"Sand dollars," I said, "I wish I could actually see one." Charles told us he had some at home and he promised to bring one to school so we could see what they look like and feel their texture. It was a great moment. That is, until Charles from Charleston was leaving and said, "Ok, well. Bye girls. I gotta get home and finish my chores. Hey, will I see you tomorrow, Catherine?"

Catherine? Why would he be asking to see her tomorrow? I'm the one who has a crush on him. I'm the one who pointed out his adorable accent. I'm the one who gave him the nickname "Charles from Charleston". I couldn't believe my ears. Charles from Charleston likes… Catherine.

"Sure, I guess so. We'll both be at school tomorrow. Me and Anne," Catherine replied.

"OK. See ya." And off Charles from Charleston went.

Catherine and I just sat on our log for what seemed like forever, not saying a word to each other. What could we say? He liked her, and I liked him. This was not right. I finally decided to speak. "Well, that was weird, huh?"

"Completely weird. Beyond weird," said Catherine.

"I guess the new boy likes the new girl. Must be your accent," I tried to joke.

"Anne, you know I would never—"

"I know, Catherine. I'm not worried about that," I lied.

"Good. Because you are the best friend I've ever had in my entire life and I would never do anything to hurt you. Even if I did like the boy."

"Wait. Do you like him?" I asked, not really wanting to hear the answer.

"No. I like… no, I don't think so. Especially not if you do."

I didn't even know what to say to that. Instead I said, "OK, well I have to get home now. I've got some chores to do." And I jumped up and ran home.

Catherine stayed on the log, looking into the creek.

CHAPTER 7
No More Secrets

I could smell dinner cooking when I got home. Beef stew. My mama could cook a mean batch of beef stew. She cut the vegetables small for me and Frank 'cause we didn't like them much and that made them so much easier to eat. Plus, there were biscuits in the oven of course. Mama was out back hanging clothes on the line and Aunt Bessie was sitting on the front porch in Mama's rocking chair, drinking sweet tea. I sat down on the front porch by her and let out a long sigh.

"Rough day today, Pumpkin?" Aunt Bessie asked.

"Yeah, pretty rough, I guess," I said.

"Wanna talk about it with your old Aunt Bessie?" she winked.

"I dunno. Not much to say," I sighed.

"Seems like a lot of hot air keeps getting trapped inside you. Maybe instead of sighing it out, you could just tell your old Aunt Bessie what's on your mind. I got two good ears, Sugar. Put'em to use."

"Aunt Bessie?"

"Yes?"

"Have you ever felt pulled between what you want and what is right?"

"Only every day of my life," Aunt Bessie laughed. "What's going on, Anne?"

"Well, I like this boy at school, Charles from Charleston. And Catherine knows I like him. And today he came to sit with us at the creek and talk. We had a great time and laughed and everything. He even promised to bring us a sand dollar to school to see."

"I love sand dollars. So, what's the problem?"

"Well, he made it very clear at the end of our talk that he likes Catherine." I heard a bump upstairs in the house. Frank must've been cleaning his room (our Thursday chore).

"Did you get mad?"

"No, not really."

"Good girl."

"But Catherine acts like she might like him. She told me she would never like him as long as I liked him. What does that even mean?"

"Sugar, that's a good friend, someone who would put aside her feelings or even her possible feelings for those of a friend. Yep, that is definitely a good friend. Don't be mad at someone when they feel something they shouldn't. Feelings come upon you like the wind. You don't see it, but you feel it the moment it hits you. Right now, she may just have a feeling. She'll know if it's real someday. But for now, it's just a feeling breezing by her. She's choosing not to grab it."

"I know, but—"

"What's going on over here, girls? Any good gossip?" It was Mama. I really didn't want to talk about this at all and now two people were here talking to me about it. "Y'all look as serious as bull with a red rug in front of it."

"Well," said Aunt Bessie, "Anne's done gone and fallen for a boy."

"Baby, I told you a thousand times, 'Don't you go wasting your heart on someone you ain't gonna marry.'"

"I know, Mama. I'm not. Honestly."

"Then what's the problem?"

"Well," said Aunt Bessie. "That boy has a crush on her friend Catherine."

"Oh. I see. Yup, that's a different story all together, now, ain't it? Well, the way I see it, Catherine is a good friend and I feel you can trust her. I can't see her doing anything about it. Her daddy would never allow her to be involved with a boy at this age, anyways. Her family is old fashioned just like ours. They have a very strict way of living, just like us. I don't think you have anything to fuss over."

"Yeah, right!" I said with a smirk.

"What was that face about? What is it, sugar?" Aunt Bessie asked.

"Nothing. It's nothing."

"What is it?" Mama demanded.

"It's just that they are not as old fashioned as you may think. That's all."

"You sound like you're speaking from experience. Anne, is there something you need to tell us?" Mama asked.

"No, of course not."

"Anne."

"It's nothing."

"ANNE!"

"I promised I would never tell a living soul."

"Anne Childers, you know you are to never keep a secret from your mama. I am the only soul that you can trust. We do not keep secrets in the Childers house. Now you spit it out. Right this minute!"

I thought long and hard. Finally, I said "OK, but you have to promise to keep it between us. I gave my word. And as you've always taught me, Mama, my word is my honesty wrapped up in sound."

"OK, Baby. You have my word."

"Well, Catherine's daddy doesn't exactly have hired people in his house."

"Sure he does, Hun. He has Virginia and Harold."

"No, Mama, he does not have hired help, he has a wife and her brother living with him."

Mama and Aunt Bessie sat there with their mouths wide open. I kept waiting for a bug to fly in and go all the way down their throats to their toes.

I can't even tell you how long we sat in silence. Mama would look at Aunt Bessie. Aunt Bessie would look at Mama. Neither one of them closed their mouths the whole time.

Finally, Aunt Bessie put her lips together, swallowed and smiled.

"Times, they are a-changin'. That's for sure. You see some of this up in Ohio. Not so much around these parts, though. Why in tarnation wouldn't they just be honest from the get-go?"

"Because they were practically run out of town in Nashville. People were ugly and said nasty things about them and threatened them. Catherine has told me all about it and it's awful."

"Well," said Mama, finally breathing again. "I guess we'll have to welcome them the right way to our town. We had no idea we were welcoming an entire family. Yes, that's what we'll have to do. Greet them proper." Mama just gazed into the woods and smiled.

Nothing else was said. Everyone forgot that my heart had been broken. All they could think about was the fact that we had us a mixed marriage in our town. It was scandalous. But Mama had always taught me that God chose people's skin, hair and eye color. And I could only hate people because of the color of their skin if I was also willing to hate them because of the color of their hair and eyes, too. So, I wasn't worried about Mama and Aunt Bessie raising a stink or gossipin' around town.

That night I went to bed feeling sad for the fact that Charles from Charleston wasn't going to be my crush anymore. But happy that I had finally shared my secret with someone. It's really heavy on a person when they have to hide something inside that long. It begins to feel like an anchor of dishonesty pulling them under to drown.

CHAPTER 8
Frank Blows It

The next day, on the way to school, I assured Catherine that I was no longer interested in Charles from Charleston and that if he wanted a girl with a backwards accent over me, well that was his choice. We both laughed, me the loudest. Maybe I was becoming more like Mama than I thought.

When we got to school, Charles said 'hey' to both of us and we said 'hey' back. Catherine gave him a smile and that's when I realized that I really didn't like Charles from Charleston, the person near as much as I liked Charles from Charleston, the idea. I was honestly OK with Catherine liking him if that's what she wanted. I was, after all, only thirteen-years-old. I would not want to waste my heart on someone I wasn't planning to marry.

At lunch me, Catherine, Margaret, Penny and Cheryl were all sitting under the big oak tree talking about a bunch of nothin' when Frank walked by. The junior high and high schools shared the same courtyard since they were on the same piece of land. Catherine said 'hi' to him with a huge grin on her face. But Frank just looked at her with a mean scowl on his face. What in the world? I had only seen Frank that mad one time and that was when the dog chewed up his baseball glove. Frank didn't even respond to Catherine. He just started to walk on, glaring at her.

"Frank! Catherine said 'hey' to you. Aren't you even going to answer back?" I asked.

"Leave me alone, Anne. This is none of your business."

What? My brother had never used that tone with me. Not even when I did things to deserve it. "Frank Childers, what in the world is wrong with you?"

"Maybe I'm the wrong color for her to want to speak to me," Frank said.

Catherine and I shot our eyes at each other. I tried to give her a look that promised I had not told him anything. We both looked back at Frank and he was just peering through her.

"Frank. What are you doing? Shut your mouth. You shut your mouth right this minute! What is wrong with you?" I said.

"Oh nothing. Just that I didn't realize that Catherine had such a colorful family. But let's be honest, no one really knows the truth now, do they?" Then he just walked away. Catherine looked at me with tears in her eyes.

"Catherine, I swear. I didn't say a word to him. I swear on my Nana's grave! Not a word!"

Margaret asked, "Say a word about what? What in the world is going on? What did Frank mean by you having a colorful family, Catherine? What did he mean he was not the right color?"

Margaret. Oh shoot. I forgot that she was even sitting there. I said that right in front of Margaret Pittman, the biggest gossiper in Bent Creek Junior High School. I threw my hand over my mouth.

"Catherine. What is going on? Is there some-thing we all need to know?" sneered Margaret. It was almost as if she was happy right now. Happy that the new, pretty girl that was liked by all (especially Charles from Charleston) was not so perfect after all. Like she'd been waiting for this moment.

"Nothing, Margaret. It's nothing. Certainly not your business." Catherine ran off.

I ran after her. She was fast, but I caught up with her. "Catherine. You have to believe me. I did not tell him anything. I swear, I did not tell him anything."

"You had to have, Anne."

"I only shared it with my mama and Aunt Bessie and that was just last night. And they would never tell him. They would never betray my trust." I said.

"Like you did mine?"

What could I say? She was right. I did betray her trust. I felt my whole body shrink.

"I swear, I did not tell him."

"Well, they told him. Or he heard you tell them. Either way, it doesn't matter, Anne. It doesn't matter because now he's started the ball rolling and I'm going to be the one trapped underneath it. Do you know what you've done? Do you see? You've ruined my life here. It's all over now. I will be everyone's joke. People will hate me. You've ruined everything, Anne. EVERYTHING!" She ran away.

I did not chase her this time. She was right. I ruined everything. I shared a secret to make myself feel better and somehow Frank found out. And now I've lost the best friend I've ever had. I had wrecked everything. But I didn't do it alone. Frank helped. I'm going to kill him!

By the end of the school day, the rumor had spread. Everyone knew that Catherine had a black stepmom. Everyone knew because my brother had a big mouth. Why would Frank be so cruel? He's never been like that before. Frank is gentle and protective. Catherine is his friend, too. He really likes her. What in the world got into him?

I ran home after school and went straight down to the creek. I didn't even do my homework or my chores. Catherine was not there. I waited for at least two hours before I ran to her house. I knocked on the door and Virginia answered. She smiled and told me that Catherine would not be able to play today. How could she even look at my face? How could she smile at me? I didn't deserve it. I'm the one that ruined their happy home, even if it was a home built on secrets.

I went home, tears pouring from my face. I had never hurt someone like this in my life. I didn't even know how to live with myself. I ran up to my room, threw myself on my bed and cried. I cried harder than I ever had before. The only saving grace of this day was that it was Friday and me and Catherine didn't have to go to school tomorrow and face people.

CHAPTER 9

The Shed

An hour later, Mama called us down to dinner. Daddy always sat at the head of the table. I sat beside Mama and Frank sat beside Aunt Bessie. I was across from Frank. I just sat there and stared a hole straight through him. I was secretly hoping that fire would shoot from my eyes and burn him up right then and there. I would not feel one bit sorry for him if it did. Not one bit!

"What in tarnation is going on with you two?" Mama asked.

"Why don't you ask Frank that question, Mama? He seems to have no problem shooting his mouth off to people lately. Right, Frank?" I said.

"Anne Childers, what's gotten into you that you would talk so cross, young lady?"

"Seriously, Mama. Ask the big bully here. He loves telling everyone what's going on. He loves spreading bad news! It makes him feel like a big man."

Frank looked down at his plate then. He knew Mama was going to ask and he knew he'd have to tell her.

"Frank, honey. What's going on?"

Frank wouldn't even speak. What a coward. I was so angry, I was shaking.

I blurted out, "Frank called out Catherine today for having a black stepmom and humiliated her in front of the whole school. He humiliated her, and she ran away. And I know she'll never speak to me again and she hates me. He ruined everything! EVERYTHING!"

Everyone sat in silence for a few seconds, then Mama blurted out, "Frank Childers, please tell me that I am not hearing this correctly. Please, Frank. Please tell me that I did not raise someone to embarrass and humiliate another person."

Frank just kept staring down at his plate of food.

That's when Mama lit up like a firecracker. She started ranting. Non-stop. It was all one big mess of angry words with no breaths in between. "Frank Childers, I tried to raise kids who love and accept others. I did not raise you to be cruel. Are you listening to me? Do you not have kindness in your heart? You know that God made our hair color, our eye color AND our skin color. Stop staring at that plate and look at me, young man. What in tarnation is wrong with you? How could you be so merciless? This certainly is not what a gentleman would do. Sit up straight, boy, I'm talking you. Who do you think you are? I cannot believe what I am hearing. I am completely beside myself right now." She just kept yelling.

About that time, Daddy spoke, and when Daddy speaks, everyone shuts up. Even Mama. "Frank, son. Am I to understand it right that my boy, my only son, humiliated a girl?"

"Yessir."

"And am I to understand it right that you called someone out for being different than you?"

"Yessir."

"And am I to understand it that you shared something private in a public setting?"

"Yessir." Frank dropped his head.

"On purpose?"

"Yessir."

"Knowing that it could ruin her?"

"Yessir." Frank slumped even lower.

"Well, Son. I think it's time you met me in the shed."

"Yessir."

Frank walked outside to the shed. Shoulders slumped, face cropped, eyes already crying a little. Serves him right. He earned a trip to the shed. I hope Daddy tears him up. I hope Daddy wallops him. I hope daddy beats him.

"Anne," said Daddy.

"Yessir?"

"You may go out there with me."

"Um. Yessir."

Why did he want me to go out there with him? Was I supposed to watch? Was I going to get a good whip at Frank? Was he going to whip me, too? What was going on?

I got to the shed and Frank was sitting there crying. He saw me come in and immediately said, "Anne. I'm so sorry. I'm so very, very sorry."

"Why, Frank? Why would you hurt Catherine like that? Why would you do that? It's not like you at all. She's your friend, for God's sake."

"I know, Anne. But last night I heard you talking to Mama and Aunt Bessie. My window was open and it's right above the porch."

"OK. Fine, but why does this bother you so much? You don't care about the color of people's skin. You've told me that before. You're the kindest boy I know. Catherine is your friend. You really like her."

"It actually doesn't bother me at all. It's just that, well, you're right, I really like Catherine. I mean, I REALLY like Catherine. I was going to ask her to the school dance this weekend. And then I heard you say she liked another boy and I just got mad. Madder than I've ever been. I don't know what came over me. I can't even believe what I've done. I was just so angry. It all just got away with me."

About that time, we noticed Daddy. How long had he been standing there? Frank stiffened up and looked at him with fear in his eyes. Daddy stood there forever before finally speaking,

"Frank, I have never been more disappointed in you than I am this very moment. You have let down this family, but more importantly you have let yourself down and you have hurt a very kind family and a very special and scared young lady. You have also ruined your sister's best friendship. And it's for that reason that I'm going to let your sister decide your punishment."

Frank and I stared at each other. Frank looked fearful and I was in shock. I have never held such power in my hands. I could have Daddy take the belt to Frank. I could have Frank do all my chores for a year. I could do so many things. But what was the right thing to do? What was I supposed to decide?

I thought for a long time. It was silent in that shed. Daddy did not rush me, he let me think it all over. Frank is my brother and I love him, but he hurt Catherine. No matter what he meant to do, he hurt her deeply. And he hurt me. But it was only because he was hurt. And now I know what that feels like. You speak before you think and somehow wind up with a big, huge foot in your mouth. My decision was made.

"Well, Daddy. If I'm the judge and the jury of this, then I decide to pardon Frank."

Daddy smiled big at me and scooped me up in his arms. "My sweet little girl! What a beautiful young woman you have become. You chose grace over justice and love over hate. I am so proud of you." He held me for the longest time. That is the closest I had ever felt to my daddy.

Then he turned to Frank. "Young man, you are very fortunate that your sister did not decide to respond to you when she was hurt the way you responded to Catherine when you were hurt."

"Yessir."

"And while she has pardoned you from punishment, this pardon does not completely let you off Scott-free. You WILL go to the Catherine's home. Tonight. You will apologize and explain how you will right this wrong you have done. You will figure a way to make this all right with her. And finally, you will do your sister's chores for a whole month. And you can count this as a favor, because I have a good mind to beat your butt with a hickory switch all the way from here to Texas."

"Yessir."

We all walked back into the house, sat down and finished dinner. While we were eating, I felt something strange building in me. I had a sense of pride moving deep inside my bones. I felt warm. I felt strong. I felt older. It was as if

I had aged ten years in the last thirty minutes. It felt good to make the right decision over the decision that felt right. It felt good to love my brother rather than punish him. The way Frank was looking at me as we ate dinner made my heart feel full. From that moment on, everything changed with me and Frank. We were different to each other. We were friends.

CHAPTER 10
Frank Spills the Beans

After dinner, Daddy said it was time for me, him and Frank to head over to the Singleton house. Mama wanted to go, but Daddy was very clear that this was Frank's doing and Frank was going to fix it.

When we got to Catherine's house, Daddy made Frank knock on the door and stand in front of us all. Virginia answered and said, "Yes. May I help you?"

We just stood there in silence until Daddy nudged Frank in the back.

"Yes, ma'am. I was wondering if you and your brother and your husband and Catherine would please take a moment to speak with me." Virginia looked surprised and then grinned out of the corners of her mouth at my daddy.

"Why yes, I think we might be able to do that. Let me check."

We waited a long time at the front door. Finally, Mr. Singleton came to the door and apologized for keeping us waiting and invited us in. We went to the parlor and sat down.

Their parlor was fancy. The couch had ornate curves on it and they had a beautiful hutch with lots of fine china in it. I'd been to Catherine's house a million times, but I'd never been in the parlor. I'd never seen anyone display their dishes like it was art. I liked it. And they had a grandfather clock that looked like it was a hundred years old, but it was still shiny.

No one knew where to begin, except Daddy that is. Daddy sat there staring at Frank. Frank was stuck. He was stuck like he was standing in mud after a rainstorm. He tried to start talking, but every time he did the words just wouldn't come out. He began to cry a little. I couldn't take it any longer, so I jumped in.

"Catherine. I'm so sorry. I'm so very, very sorry! I betrayed your trust in me as a friend. I should have never told my mama and Aunt Bessie your secret. It was wrong of me and I hope that someday you can forgive me. You are the best friend I've ever had. I'm so ashamed I let you down."

It was at this time that Mr. Singleton spoke up and said, "My daughter should never have made you keep a secret. It was unfair of her to ask you to hold on to something that would weigh you down so heavily. Something that maybe you would need to discuss with an adult to help you understand it more. We have discussed it with her, and she realizes that it was not fair to you."

"I'm sorry, Anne. I didn't realize that I was making it hard for you. I had no idea the pressure I was putting on you. I just needed a friend to know the real me. I didn't mean to put such a burden on you."

"I'm sorry, too Catherine. I'm just so sorry." We looked at each other with a hug in our eyes, but we both knew this was not the time for that right now. Frank still had to say whatever it was that he came to say.

After a little nudging from Daddy, Frank spoke. "Catherine, Mr. and Mrs. Singleton, Mr. Harold, I want to apologize for embarrassing your family and for saying things that I didn't even mean. It was cruel of me and hurtful and I can't believe I did it. My mama and Daddy raised me not to judge others by the color of their skin and I never have. Not even when I said it. I said it because I was mad and hurt. I didn't mean it. I know I can't take away what I've done, but I will work hard to right my wrong. I will protect Catherine from people when we go back to school on Monday. I will not let anyone say anything to her. I will stay by her side."

"Frank, why?" Catherine finally blurted out, tears streaming down her cheeks. "Why would you say that? Why would you do that? If you honestly didn't care and if it really wasn't a big deal to you? Why, Frank? I thought we were friends. I thought we liked each other. You said you were hurt. What did I ever do to you that would make you hurt me so much? I cannot think of one mean or cruel thing I've ever done to you. Not one."

I think Frank sat there for at least two minutes in silence. He kept opening his mouth, but the words didn't make it past his tongue.

"Frank!" Daddy snapped. So loud that Catherine, Frank and I, all three, jumped a little. Then the words spilled out of him like Daddy had been in his throat just-a-pushin.

"Because, Catherine, I like you. I've liked you from the day I met you. I know I'm two years older and I know we're young, but I like you to the point that I just know someday we are going to get married. I wasn't mad about your secret either. I know people are mean and that's why you kept it. I was mad because you liked 'Charles from Charleston' and it hurt me. I reacted wrong and I'm ashamed. I'm so ashamed and I'm sorry." Frank suddenly froze, realizing he had just spilled his guts all over the place. He was embarrassed and nervous. It served him right.

We all sat in silence. My dad and Mr. Singleton with smirks on their faces. And Virginia holding Catherine's hand and petting her. No one really knew what to say or when to say something. We waited and waited until finally Catherine spoke out.

"Well, Frank, you have a very peculiar way of getting a girl's attention." We all burst out laughing. All of us, that is, except Harold. Harold just sat there staring at Frank.

Daddy looked at Harold, stood up and said, "Harold, I want you to know that I am genuinely sorry for my son bringing trouble to your family.

I know that this union is not your choice, but your sister's. And that's a lot of load for a man to carry without volunteering. But I see it this-a-way. You are a good, honest man who has stood beside his family through thick and thin. And when I say we want to be a part of helping the Singleton family be accepted into our community, I include you in that statement. You will be as much a friend to the Childers family as the rest of your kin. I would be honored to stand beside such a strong and courageous and faithful man as yourself."

It was at that statement that Harold stood up, tears in his eyes and shook my daddy's hand. "I thank you very much, Mr. Childers. You are certainly a fine man."

Finally, Virginia spoke, "Well, I guess you three will have a bit of work to get through the next few weeks at school. But, as for me, I can honestly say, I'm thankful it's out and that we don't have to pretend anymore. I did not choose to marry this man so that I could hide our love in the walls of this house. He is my husband and I am proud of that. There will always be people who won't accept us. But I didn't marry him for acceptance. I married him because I love him and want to spend the rest of my life with him. We will all get through this."

We stood up. There was nothing left to say after that. Virginia had said it all, or so I thought.

"Frank," Daddy said.

"Yessir?"

"Isn't there a question you wanted to ask Catherine?"

"Uh... Would you please forgive me?"

"Yes, Frank. Of course. I understand what you were feeling. I do."

"Frank."

"Yessir?"

"That's not the question I was talking about."

"I don't understand, sir," said Frank, baffled.

"You know. The question you were going to ask before you got wounded like a puppy and reacted like a donkey." Yep, Daddy had heard everything in the shed.

Frank blushed. He had already humiliated himself enough. But Daddy was egging him on even more. Serves him right.

"Um, Catherine?"

"Yes, Frank."

"Well, there's a dance next week at the high school and I was wondering if you'd go with me." Frank looked like he was about the throw up all over their couch.

Catherine thought for a bit and then said, "No, Frank. I will not go with you to the dance. You see, I've liked you since the day I met you, too. But I figured you were too old for me and thought I was just a little girl. But now that I know you like me, I think I'll make you work for it. If we are, after all, going to marry someday. I need to let you know from the beginning that you cannot push me around or bully me to get your way."

"Fair enough" said Frank, with a wry, crooked smile forming at the corner of his mouth. Catherine blushed. How did I not see this all along?

CHAPTER 11
The Three Musketeers

Monday morning came quicker than Catherine, Frank or I wanted it to. But we were now a united force. We were determined not to let what others said or thought bring us down or come between us, ever again.

Frank walked us to school that day (and every day after that.) When we got to school, I saw Cheryl, Penny and Margaret standing by the front stairs staring at us. Margaret, of course was gabbing on about something and I was pretty sure I knew what. So, I took Catherine's hand and we walked right up to them. The red rug was attacking the bull this time.

"Hey girls!" I said a little too eagerly.

"Did you hear something?" asked Margaret.

"Yes, you heard me, Margaret Pittman. And you are not too good to speak back to me, no matter what you think of yourself."

"Oh. My. Goodness!" screeched Margaret as she walked off. Penny, of course, followed right along.

As Cheryl stood there, not really knowing what the right thing was to do, I said to her, "Cheryl. You have a chance, right now at thirteen years of age to make your own decision for once in your life. You can keep following someone who has never really cared about you or you can stand here with us for what is right. Stand here with your friends who would never tell you how to think or feel but allow you to determine that yourself."

Cheryl stood there for a while and finally said, "Well now, Anne Childers, that was a beautiful speech. But I don't need your permission to choose my friends, thank you very much." I felt horrible. Then I looked up at Cheryl and she was grinning. She threw her arm around me and Catherine and we walked into school together.

From that day on we were the three musketeers. Margaret and Penny tried to get under our skin every now and then, but the truth is, if you don't respect a person, their negative opinion of you doesn't really hurt that much.

CHAPTER 12
The High School Years

F rank was as good as his word. He did everything within his power to protect Catherine.
He never let anyone make fun of her or her
family. Of course, people tried. But not all
people. Not everyone is bad. Once a boy named
Theo Gainer tried to ruffle some feathers. We
had gone to the hardware store to get some
supplies and we heard Theo say, "Look, Mama.
It's them nigger-lovers." I thought I was going
to slug him right there in the store, in front of
God and everybody. Pow, right in the throat. I
saw Daddy start to walk over when Frank put
his hand on Daddy's shoulder, stopping him.

Frank walked right over to Theo and said,
"I'm sorry that it's hard for you to accept that
there are other kind of people in this world
besides yourself. But if I were you, I'd watch
my mouth. You understand?"

Theo stared at Frank and Frank did not move a muscle. Finally, Theo said, "Why? What you gonna do about it." I'm pretty sure I saw Theo's lip shaking and it was covered with sweat.

"I'm gonna help you shut up if you can't figure it out on your own."

"Well, I never," said Theo's mama.

"You really should keep your boy in line," she said to my daddy. And then she and Theo stormed off. Daddy just guffawed about that for weeks. Said his boy was a man among men and next time he needed a bodyguard, he was calling Frank.

Frank did eventually get to go to a dance with Catherine and she wore the second most beautiful dress I'd ever seen. It was pink and green and had a big, puffy tulle skirt underneath it. Every time she spun around, she looked like a real-life princess. She and Frank got the stares, of course, but they didn't pay any attention to it. Me and Cheryl stayed close by. We were kinda each other's dance date every time there was a dance. Since we'd decided to stand by Catherine and her family, people weren't as nice and easy-going with us as they should have been. But as long as we had each other, we had a blast.

Those next few years were hard at times, but mostly they were wonderful. Catherine, Frank and I continued to have fun together. We went for long walks and spent most of our time talking in the tree house.

Our first year of high school was amazing and we had so much fun dressing up and looking and talking older. Mama didn't like it all that much, me getting older and dressing older. There were several times she made me change my clothes after I walked downstairs. That usually happened when I borrowed some of Catherine's clothes. It was the strangest thing, she never judged Catherine for wearing them, but she held the law down on me when it came to my wardrobe. She'd always say, "Boys see enough beyond what your wearing to make up for what you're not showing. Let's keep their imaginations in check, why don't we." Oh Mama, I love her!

There were lots of people in school that tried to give Catherine a hard time, but with me and Frank and Cheryl there, it wasn't that bad. And after a couple of years, it almost didn't exist. Don't get me wrong, there will always be a Margaret, a Penny and a Theo in life. Especially a Margaret. I can't exactly tell you why, but they just aren't happy unless they are making people miserable. But, like I said, their opinion doesn't weigh heavy on you when you don't respect them.

Frank and Catherine did become so much more than friends. The older they got, the closer they became. I didn't really mind so much. I knew that there was no way to stop that train from running down the track, so I might as well jump on and enjoy the ride. And I'm so glad I did. I found out more about my brother, my best friend and myself by enjoying their journey with them. Yep, Frank and I really did have a change with each other that night in the shed and we were friends for life. I imagine we will be like Mama and Aunt Bessie, going to each other's houses and watching each other raise kids and do life.

When we got into the 11th grade, Frank was no longer there to protect Catherine. That year, Margaret, Penny and Penny's boyfriend, Charles (yep, you guessed it, Charles from Charleston) really tried to get under our skin, but by then, they couldn't. I'm pretty sure that year was so much harder for them because by that time we were used to it all and had our minds in other places. Catherine was always thinking of Frank. Cheryl and I were thinking of what we wanted to do with our lives. Women had the power to determine their own future now and we were going to set our own paths.

It was that year in senior high school that a man named Martin Luther King, Jr. gave a speech in Washington, D.C. encouraging us to treat all people of all religions and all colors equally. It was what people called the beginning of change in our country. I like to think we played a small role in that change. Dr. King's speech touched me and made me think about making a change in more than just a small spot on the map. I wanted to make a change in the world. It made me think about courage and hate and love and independence and influence. I decided at that point that whatever I did with my future, it would involve helping people to have the courage to stand up for what is right. I talked with my teacher, Mrs. Middlebrooks and she said she had always thought I'd be a great teacher.

A teacher? I had never even considered it. How in the world could someone like me take on such an important role in life? I mean, teachers are the ones that set peoples' directions. They are the ones that teach people respect and honor and compassion. They are the ones that help people find their way when they are lost. They are the ones that inspire and motivate. They are the ones who prove to people that they are so much more than they think. YES! That is what I wanted to be. Mrs. Middlebrooks saw a gift in me. She knew. She saw. She knew that in order to make a change, I would need to be in a position where I could impact others. It was that year that I decided to become a teacher. That was how I was going to change the world. One person at a time.

I ran home that day after school. I didn't even wait for Catherine or Cheryl. I couldn't wait to tell Mama what I had decided. I knew she'd laugh and scream and tell me exactly how to follow my dreams. As soon as I walked in the door, I told Mama and to my shock, she didn't jump out of her seat and tell me what a fabulous idea that was and how she knew it all along. Instead, she started crying. I had rarely seen either of my parents cry. Mama cried when her Mama died. Daddy cried that day in the shed. But my parents just weren't criers. So, I sat there and stared at her, not knowing what to say. I figured this was one of those times that you sit and give a person some space and time to gather their thoughts so they can tell you clearly what they think. After a long wait, it seemed like a half an hour, Mama spoke.

"Sugar, I have never felt so much pride and fear in the same moment. I have always known that you had wings underneath your skin waiting to be let out. But I also always hoped you wouldn't find them. Because with wings you fly and I'm not ready for you to fly away from me. And I know you won't be learning to be a teacher out here on the land with us. How will I ever let you take one step away from me on a journey that will probably never bring you back?" And then she sat there and cried.

In my whole life, I had never felt that close to my mama. I had never felt so connected. The moment she said it, I knew it was true. I'd leave her, Daddy, Frank, Catherine and Cheryl. I'd go out into the world and I'd find my own way of doing things. And I was thrilled! Thrilled and petrified. And feeling strong.

I pulled my chair over beside Mama, placed my hand over hers and told her, "This is how you raised me. This is who you taught me to be. A woman with purpose, meaning and courage. I can make a difference and I can help people. I want to help people. Mama, do you hear me? I want to help people. I learned that from you!" We embraced and held each other like it was the last time we would ever be in the same room.

Later that night I heard her tell Daddy and his response shocked me too, "I always knew Frank would take over the land and the business and maybe travel a bit, but I thought my Anne would marry locally and stay close by." How did Mama get that I had wings and Daddy didn't even have a clue?

My senior year was fun and sad. Catherine, Cheryl and I had a blast doing all the fun things high-schoolers do, but we knew in the back of our minds that we'd never be the same after this year. I was going to go to university to become a teacher. Cheryl had no clue what she was doing, and Frank and Catherine were already talking about marriage. We took everything we could out of that year and made it our best year ever.

CHAPTER 13
The Big Day

I stayed home for the first year after senior high. We had a wedding to plan and a house to build for Frank and Catherine. And in 1967, Catherine walked down the aisle to marry my brother, Frank Childers. That was the day she wore the absolute, most beautiful dress I'd ever seen. She was stunning. As usual she stood out among a crowd. Her wedding dress was satin with lace along the edges. It was bell shaped. And her veil. Oh, her veil! It poofed out behind her like a halo. Aunt Bessie got to come for the wedding. Harold had passed away a year earlier in a car accident. Catherine put a picture of him in a chair beside Virginia on the front row.

Frank and Catherine Childers now live on our beautiful land with their three children. Frank never changed a thing. Daddy was right, it is perfect just the way it is!

During my first year in college, in 1968, someone murdered Martin Luther King, Jr. for standing up for what he believed in. I was outraged. I was broken. I was mourning. I wanted to do something but had no idea what to do. Over the next year, I struggled to find my voice as to how to respond. One day, while chatting with a friend on campus, she told me about a third-grade teacher in an all-white Christian school in Iowa named Jane Elliott. Ms. Elliott led her students in an experiment on eye-color discrimination. In this study, Ms. Elliott demonstrated how the children who were considered superior because of their eye color gave in to discriminatory and judgmental behavior based on nothing more than being told they were superior because they had brown eyes. Not only that, but it was also scientifically proven that the same chemical that gives skin it's color, Melanin, is also the same chemical that give eyes and hair their color. I guess Mama was right after all! You really can't judge skin color unless you're willing to judge eye and hair color, too. I knew I would use this knowledge one day in my class. I would use this lesson to educate and inspire and break the chains of racism and hate and to empower people to have strength and courage to stand up for what is right and to love others without prejudice.

In 1972, I finally got to marry Charles. Charles from Texas, that is. I met Charles Kirkpatrick at the University of South Carolina where I earned my B.A. in education.

I will never forget that profound year of my life and the lessons I learned from it. It changed my view of people, perceptions and friendship. It changed my perspective of myself. I hope that I can pass that on to my students. It has become my life's mission.

EPILOGUE
Home Again

1980:

"This is the smoothest train I've ever been on," Charles said.

"I know, and they even serve 'fried chicken' for breakfast on it," I replied as I cut my eggs. We both laughed. Of course, I had shared that story with my husband many times as it is one of my favorites about my mama.

Emma, who was eight at the time, was not listening to us. She was staring out the window taking in all the beautiful scenery. Also, she had heard that story a million times and I think it has lost its humor with her by now.

The conductor was passing by and Charles asked him when we would arrive. He looked at his watch and said that since we were running on time, we should arrive in about 15 minutes. My heart started racing. This would be my first time home in three years. Charles and I had a lot of settling to do when we moved for his job to Texas. And Texas is a long ways away to visit all the time. It costs a lot of money and takes tons of planning. The last time I visited home was three years ago and it was without Charles. It was just me and Emma. I swore I'd never leave Charles for that long again. No matter how much I missed Mama and Daddy and Frank and Catherine, I missed my husband even more. So, we saved our money and here we are, fifteen minutes away.

The train pulled into the station and I could hear the brakes rubbing the tracks. I remembered back to all the times we would wait to pick up Aunt Bessie.

We got off the train and I ran into Mama's arms. She was crying and so was I.

I hugged my daddy with all that was in me. And then I made eye contact with Catherine. I could hardly hold myself back from embracing her. She was so much more than a friend now. We were sisters. We talked on the phone weekly and shared our lives, even if it was long distance. After that, I turned to my brother, who had long since become my friend and we embraced. Then I hugged my nephews and my niece, and they began chatting away with Emma.

We got our luggage and headed out to the parking lot and I smiled as I passed through the now renovated train station that made no mention of a person's color. What a refreshing change it was from my childhood in this sleepy town.

After we got home and settled in at Frank and Catherine's house, I watched as Emma, Monica and the boys ran off to the woods. Here is my child running into my woods with my brother and my best friend's kids. What a beautiful sight that was. As I looked around, taking in the beauty of my childhood memories, I noticed that about a half an acre had been cleared off in the back. When I asked Daddy, he told me that he and Mama had grown tired of climbing up and down stairs and they were building a small house for them to downsize into.

"But what about our house? What are you going to do with it.?" I asked.

"Well," said Frank. "It's too small for my family. I guess we don't know yet what we're going to do with it." Then we all waked into Frank and Catherine's house.

Catherine, Frank, Charles and I sat down in the living room and caught up on old times while Mama and Daddy went home to their house to take care of a few things. Frank was acting particularly silly the whole time we were chatting. I had no idea what was going on with him. He was being so peculiar. After a couple of hours of catching up, it was finally time to start preparing dinner. So, Mama, Catherine and I started to get things ready while Daddy, Frank and Charles headed outside. Daddy wanted to show Charles some of the changes he'd made in the old house. When Frank and Catherine got married, Daddy and Frank built a new house on the property for them to live in. But now that Mama and Daddy were downsizing, they had one house too many and were probably going to tear down the house that I grew up in. My heart was secretly breaking over the idea. But it wasn't mine to do with.

We called the kids in at 6:00 for dinner. The adults sat at the big table and the kids sat at the fold out table, all crammed together. As I watched them laugh and joke with each other, my heart ached for Emma to know her cousins better.

Over dinner Frank and Mama asked me lots of questions. If I liked where I was living. If I liked the school where I was teaching. If Emma was involved in lots of activities. I answered them all and noticed that they kept inwardly laughing after I answered each question. I liked our neighborhood just fine. Emma was not really involved in any activities out there, we are still trying to figure out what she loved most, theater, singing or writing. I liked the school OK. But I really felt I wasn't making a difference like I'd hoped to. And with each answer, Frank and Mama would chuckle and Daddy and Catherine would get silly grins on their faces and stare at each other.

"OK, that's it. What in the world is going on with you, Frank Childers? And you, Mama. What is going on here? You have all been acting strange and silly this whole day."

"Haven't they always been that way?" said Catherine.

"Ha ha," replied Frank, sarcastically.

"Maybe I can answer that question for him," said Charles. Wait, what? Charles? What did he have to do with Frank acting so crazy today?

"OK. Enlighten me. What in tarnation is going on."

"Well," started Charles, "I have been doing so great at my job and I honestly couldn't be happier than I am now. With both my job and my family."

"OK..." I said.

"And, well. They are just as happy with me, too. And they've offered me a promotion. I'm moving to upper management! I'm so excited. This is good for us financially and we won't struggle as much to see your family anymore."

"That's wonderful, Charles. I'm so proud of you!" I cheered. Charles began to tell us all about his new position. What his title would be and what he'd be doing and how much more money he'd be making.

Finally, it dawned on me that he had shared this news with everyone else before he shared it with me. "Wait. But why did you tell all of them before you told me?" I asked. It was not like Charles at all to share something so private with someone else before me.

"Well, I had to make sure that I spoke with your parents and checked with Frank and Catherine to be sure they wouldn't mind if we lived in your old house."

"I…. I don't understand."

"Honey, the new job is here! It will be a little bit of a drive from the country for me, but I can't think of place you'd be happier than right here with your family."

Tears began pouring down my face. Not just mine, but Catherine's, Frank's and Mama's as well. Charles was no crier, but I swear I saw his eyes fill with water.

I ran over to him and just held him in my arms. This husband of mine was such a gift. I was finally going to be home again. My feet hardly touched the ground the rest of the evening.

Later that evening after Mama and Daddy had gone back to their house, Charles, Frank, Catherine and I were sitting out on the front porch drinking sweet tea as the kids talked up a storm in the tree house. Suddenly Monica and Emma came running up to us and Monica had tears in her eyes. Emma then told us Mark had said something ugly to Monica and hurt her feelings. We called the boys over and talked it all out and Mark apologized. Then he said to his daddy, "Did you and Aunt Anne ever fight like this."

"Goodness no!" said Frank, far too dramatically.

We all laughed and I sat back in my chair, took a big gulp of my tea and said, "Kids, have I ever told you about the time your daddy was taken to the shed when he got in trouble and your Papaw actually gave me the choice of what his punishment would be?" The kids stared at me wide-eyed and said, "Tell us, Aunt Anne!" I rocked a bit in my chair and Frank smiled at me. I pictured my Aunt Bessie and Mama sitting on the old porch and could hear them laughing. I began, "One day…"

Acknowledgements:

I am so grateful to my husband, Jonathan for always believing I was more than I believed I could be. I did it!

Thank you to my children, Jake, Alex and Zach, for allowing me to always tell stories in the most dramatic ways. Without wanting to tell you the fried chicken scene, I never would have started this book.

Thank you to my parents, Gary and Brenda Phillips for pushing me to follow an impossible dream. Your belief in me gave me courage.

Thank you to all my friends and family who encouraged me all the way through this process.

Thank you to Wendie Appel, from Purple Finch Press, for taking a chance on a total stranger. Your act of kindness is, in all reality, the only reason a first step was taken.